I0640699

Martin F. Tupper

Washington

a drama, in five acts

Martin F. Tupper

Washington
a drama, in five acts

ISBN/EAN: 9783337344016

Printed in Europe, USA, Canada, Australia, Japan

Cover: Foto ©Andreas Hilbeck / pixelio.de

More available books at **www.hansebooks.com**

WASHINGTON:

A DRAMA, IN FIVE ACTS.

BY

MARTIN F. TUPPER,

D.C.L.. OXFORD: AND F.R.S.

Author of Proverbial. Philosophy, Alfred, Raleigh,
Crock of Gold, &c., &c.

———

Written for the Centenary of American Independence in
honour of its founder. Not yet published in England.

———

NEW YORK:

JAMES MILLER, PUBLISHER.

1876.

NOTICE.

This Play will be read in public by the author during his present visit to America.

Condensation of the incidents of a lifetime within the limits of an hour or two needs must involve leaps between act and act, and gaps from scene to scene; but it is hoped nevertheless that the narration flows on naturally. My work has been a very rapid labour of love, but still a labour, and no indolent outpouring of extemporary fancies; seeing there will be found due historical authority for most of the incidents, and a fair amount of truthful consistency pervading all the characters; everywhere, an intelligent auditor, who is conversant with Washington and his times, will detect touches of quotation from celebrated speeches, and allusions to famous anecdotes. It will be remembered that biographers sometimes contradict each other (indeed a single one would always be sufficient, if his facts were undisputed), and that the writer of a play from such materials must select the most picturesque points and make the best of them.

Having all through my life had an honest admiration for George Washington [in a very early book of mine, "The Modern Pyramid," he is one of my "Worthiest of Mankind"], I rejoice in the chance of making a monogram of his noble life: and my own well-known international sentiments now for nearly half a century, dating as they do ancestrally from much older times, will be a good excuse, if such be needed, for producing this Play on the Centenary of American Independence.

Appropriate music for the overture and Entr'actes, if by possibility it comes to be dramatically represented, might be some well-managed olio of international tunes, arranged to be in keeping with the libretto of each act; and the dresses must of course be of the period. Washington as President (act 1 sc. 2) first appears in his conventional black velvet, and the deputies in court dress. Afterwards his changes will be the dress and undress uniforms of an American General in 1776.

The play being a short one, and every line well considered, the author hopes it will be acted as written, without excisions or insertions.

It may be as well to state with respect to the national

flag (act 2 sc. 3), that the incident at Mount Vernon oc-
curred to myself, and that I long after verified the matter
at Herald's College: in May, 1851, I announced it to the
Historical Society at Baltimore, who paid me the compli-
ment of their diploma thereupon, after a public dinner,
with Mr. Kennedy as chairman, and Sir Henry Bulwer
and the present writer as his supports. Washington's
original coat — as explained by Franklin — can be copied
from Herald's College and possessed by any one for a
small fee: an engraving thereof is on the outer title of
this Play.

About the quasi-Corday incident, I have only invented
as to sex; for Washington's life was more than once at-
tempted, and he excused the culprits. It was also per-
missible for me to suppose his earliest love — the unknown "lowland beauty" — to have been Arnold's sister;
and I may add that it is not only likelihood but truth,
that Washington's wife frequently accompanied him in
his campaigns, especially at Valley Forge.

Some knowledge of the subject is presupposed in a dis-
cerning and enlightened audience on either side of the
Atlantic. I would not weight the action of the play with
more than could be helped of explanatory matter, nor
overlay its incidents with the petty and prosaic details of
conflicting testimony. It may be as well to state that,

although I have lately heard of several plays on the great name "Washington," I have seen none of them; if any similarities are perceptible, they are accidental, and due probably to an honest use of the like materials by the several authors: history must not be originally invented.

With this preface, Reader, I commend my drama of "Washington" to your favour.

MARTIN F. TUPPER.

ALBURY, 1875.

CHARACTERS.

WASHINGTON.

BENJAMIN FRANKLIN.

PATRICK HENRY.

JOHN ADAMS.

BENEDICT ARNOLD, the traitor.

Marquis LA FAYETTE.

Major ANDRÉ, the spy.

Corporal THOMPSON.

DEACON ELDAD.

NATHAN, a Quaker.

BISHOP, Washington's Bodyservant.

TIMOTHY.

MARTHA WASHINGTON.

MARY ARNOLD.

RACHEL, her maid.

WASHINGTON.

ACT I.

SCENE 1. — *The Quay at Boston; enter at opposite points* DEACON ELDAD, *and* NATHAN, *with others.*

NATHAN.

Is he come back? who knoweth? and what tidings?

ELDAD.

One question at a time, friend: shrewd Ben Franklin
Came by this packet, — and the Morning Star
They say had full seven weeks of it, for storms,
And calms, and contrary winds, — but as to news
Nothing known yetawhile: he holds his tongue,
That wise old proverb-monger, for he thinks
" Least said is soonest mended ; " which I doubt,
For if one would expound, —

NATHAN.

        But touching England?
What message is brought back from our hard mother?
Who knoweth? guesseth aught?

9

ELDAD.

Patience awhile:
To-day the Congress meets; we shall soon hear
How Franklin sped before the King in Council,

(enter ARNOLD*)*

And with what favour or what bitter speech
Old England greets her ancient colonies, —

NATHAN.

Pray heaven she speak us fair, —

ARNOLD.

By heaven, she'd better!
Or from the fists of her own freeborn sons
She shall be taught that tyrants cannot rule them:
What? shall our mother, — call her step-mother, —
Tax us against our wills, strangle our trade,
Force on us reams of her extortionate stamps,
Shut up our chapels and our printing presses,
Make laws to bind us (no leave asked or given),
Set judges over us, but we to pay,
Deny us jury-trial, that old free right,
Quarter an army here at our own cost,
To keep us down in case we dared to rise, —
By heaven! but England shall deal thus no longer!

NATHAN.

Stranger, our King is just, ay generous,
Can do no wrong, nor will it: and his rights,
Taxing, protecting, governing, and binding,
May not be touched — as of the Lord's Anointed.

ARNOLD.

A suffering people, not their somewhile tyrant,
Such be the Lord's anointed!

ELDAD.

Yet we, friend,
Be subjects still, and must obey the laws, —
For look you —

ARNOLD.

Hold! — obey them, if we make them;
Not else: if made against our wills, or worse
Without our freeborn voices in contempt,
They are no laws to us; subjects, not slaves,
His Majesty's right loyal colonists
(Be it as you will) — yet independent, free,
Safe to give all due honour, homage, custom,
But scorning to be mulcted in our right, —

NATHAN.

And wouldst thou have us rebels for such right?
If right it be for men to rule themselves.

ARNOLD.

Predestined slave! a man is not a man
Who suffers any rule that thwarts his will.
Those who let others govern as they please,
Without the votes of freemen freely given,
Are but the meanest cowards: none such here.

ELDAD.

This smells like treason, sir, for —

ARNOLD.

Treason be it!
If George of England steals the rights of man,
George of America shall win them back.
Ay, let the King, if he must mutter thunders,
Beware lest our Ben Franklin draw down lightning,
And such a storm be raised shall split the globe,
Riving it that the two halves stand apart.

NATHAN.

Forefend that evil day.

ARNOLD.

No! let it come!
Our millions must be free; it is high time;
Too long has England drained us well nigh dry,
Her milch-kine colonists, and worse than so,
Sucking our lifeblood with her vampyre lips, —
Then welcome Revolution!

NATHAN.

That were ruin,
Spoiling all gainful commerce every way;
What though some liberties be bound, what if
The candles of some consciences are dimmed?
We still may light the lamps of industry
And earn by merchandize all man can want;
I'm not for war, — nor freedom, meaning war,
Nor any strife, nor patriotism, —

ARNOLD.

Shame!
Shame on your miserable peacemongering!

We must light torches of a fiercer sort
Than those dull office lamps of industry;
Torches to blaze and burn, quenched but by blood,
If any dare to touch our liberties, —

(*enter* MARY ARNOLD)

How now, my sister?

MARY ARNOLD.

Benedict, I ran
To tell you the sad news, that Major André
— So soon to be your brother and my husband, —
Has heard, and all too truly; peace and war
Hung in the balances, — and peace is down.

ARNOLD.

Then André is my foe, — and must be yours! —
A feathered gallant in the tyrant's camp
Can claim no brotherhood with me — or you —
From this day you renounce him!

MARY ARNOLD.

Never, never!
Benedict, you were always my fierce brother
Even from the day since we were both left orphans;
Yet was I plighted with your given good leave
To mine own loved John André, months agone,
And none shall part us now! for life, for death,
Mary and John are wedded as one spirit!

ARNOLD.

Tut, girl! you must forget him.

MARY.

Benedict,
My brother, be more merciful; thou knowest
I cannot, dare not stand against thy will, —
I always feel its power wrestling me down,
Yet, leave my heart its treasure!

ARNOLD.

Silly child,
I too can rave — more sternly — never, never!
If Major André fights on England's side,
He bursts the bond between us. Go, forget him, —
You shall not leave my house. Obey my will.
       (*Some run in*)   (*exit* MARY.)
Ho! Citizens : is it all blurted out?
Is the sword drawn, to strike for liberty?
Hurrah for the good news! Come, let us haste
On to this Congress, our new league the States
Headed by Washington, to hear what Franklin
Brings us from hostile England as our envoy.

SCENE 2. — *Washington in Council: deputies sitting
round: some citizens grouped behind.*

WASHINGTON.

Statesmen and brothers, we are met this day
Solemnly to proclaim our rights and wrongs,
Duteously in sober wisdom to decide,
And firmly with all promptitude to act

For peace or war, as Providence may will.
Our messenger from England, Benjamin Franklin,
Awaits your bidding, to make known to us
What the King chooses for us — and himself.

(Enter FRANKLIN. They shout)

Welcome, good brother! welcome, Benjamin Franklin!

FRANKLIN.

Worshipful President, and worthy Statesmen,
When, as the thirteen colonies resolved,
I stood your delegate and deputy
To plead our rights before King George in council,
I had small hope — it scarce was worth a fear, —
That minister or King would favour us.
Lord North was proud and cold and reticent,
The King — to speak out plainly — obstinate,
Grenville, and Grafton too, seemed full of scorn
At parleying with (for so they called us) traitors;
And though great Chatham spoke up nobly for us
As injured and unhappy and traduced,
Stoutly protesting how we well deserved
For patient patriotism to that hour
To hold all right God giveth unto man
Self-government and natural liberties
Of conscience, speech, religion, trade, all free,
Glad that we stood for them; though Edmund Burke
Made the assembled council tremble and thrill
When from his fervid heart and eloquent tongue
Our wrongs were poured before them; and though
    Barré

Flashed Junius-fire from out his cunning eyes
Whilst he denounced and lashed with irony
The placemen and the pensioners, who dared
To play the tyrant over us, — all was vain,
Our cause, I saw it at once, had been prejudged;
The die was cast; they flung my pleas aside,
They scoffed at protestation, railed at us,
As runaway emigrants, adventurers,
Nay, some (they sneered) convicted criminals,
Deserters out of bounds, plantation serfs,
His Majesty's own property forsooth,
Born but for tribute and to render dues :
Thus did they taunt us: — but I answered them;
That we were now three million honest men
Freeborn, and claiming liberty as right;
We had grown strong in our Columbian home;
And would not tolerate prætorian guards
To keep us prisoners, ay, and feed on us;
I said we hated priest-craft, and would none
Of State religion, and its hierarchy,
We would have none of foreign laws or judges
Or taskmaster officials grinding us
By tyrannous taxation everywhere, —
I told them we denounced, renounced all these,
And claimed, though loyal still, self-government.
Yet all fell through ; an utter chaos of failure
Seemed to crash round me, like a shattered world ;
And then I felt much as that self-strong man,
Horace's, you remember, — who defies
As you, with me, defy the thunderbolt
Even of tyrannic Jove himself : alone,

In the calm majesty of self-respect,
I thus threw down your gage of Independence,
And, full free conduct granted, came away
Pledged, like yourselves, a rebel for the right!

(The COUNCIL *cheer him)*

Bravo, great Franklin, — bravely spoken, brother.

WASHINGTON.

Statesmen, we all approve and countersign
The noble words and acts of Benjamin Franklin ;
Your votes by acclamation.

(They shout)

All, all, all!

WASHINGTON.

So then in sorrow, with no brutish joy
No Sea-king's love of fighting, but in view
Of all the horrid front of civil war,
Protesting but its sad necessity,
We turn and face the tyrant ; close our ports
Against his shipping, flinging overboard
His cargoes rather than pay tax for them,
Blockade his troops, self-prisoned in our forts,
Proclaiming war against the enemy,
And stand up strong before the world of men
Right glad with us to hail our independence
Thirteen as one, these new United States,
Determined to live free, — if not, to die!
The legend of our old alarum bell

Inscribed around its rim is then prophetic, —
" Proclaim ye liberty throughout the land,
" Freedom to all the inhabitants thereof !

(*The group of citizens in the rear of the* COUNCIL *cheer and
    hurrah ; outside, a great shouting and ringing of bells
    and firing cannon, &c.   The deputies, saluting Wash-
    ington, leave him alone, — he speaks*)

Thus, England, we must break away from thee :
My father's home for full four hundred years
Or ever we came here a century back,
Must be renounced for ever:
                    Be it so. —
If in this struggle I win the glorious prize
Our people's freedom to the end of time
A nation that shall overflow the globe
Making this hemisphere the fountain-head, —
Lo what a Pisgah-view to one who stands
The Father of his country, to all ages
Living in them revered : — but if I lose;
How swift and terrible the penalties!
The vast estates my honoured father left me
Forfeited, my rich revenues by marriage
Confiscate, and that best-loved wife a beggar, —
While for myself the traitor's hideous doom,
Hanged, drawn and quartered! — what a fearful price
For the mere strife to conquer liberty :
Yet must I dare it all, even that shame
For Liberty, for glorious Liberty!
The sword is drawn, the die of fate is cast;

Liberty shall be conquered if I live,
And if I die, for others let me die
In their just cause of freedom : be the past
Wiped out as dead, — the present, bloody effort,
The future dark as night.   But — what of duty,
What of obedience, what of just affection?
Are these all sure and safe on freedom's side?
Can I abjure my country, and my King,
Nor feel a parricide against a mother ? —
Mother? yet there are seen some so-called mothers
Unmotherly, harsh-featured, heavy-handed,
The callous and hard-hearted sort, in whom
Maternal instinct is all dead, while those
Counted her children, driven from hearth and home
Can no more call her blessed !   Mother ? well —
If she neglects to teach and train her sons,
Crushes their energies for selfish gain,
Makes them her serfs and drudges, keeps them down
Though they are grown, fullfledged for liberty,
When freedom is their right, — is this a mother
To taunt me with ingratitude, or claim
Parental honour ? — No ! King George's England
Has shown small mercy to her far-off sons
Exiled for conscience sake in evil days ;
And we are still fallen on days as evil
Tyrannically taxed, straitened, kept down,
Treated like children, worse, like slaves ! — O soul,
Pray hard for better times !   May some glad change
(Haply long hence — perhaps a hundred years, —
For nations move but slowly) yet find England
Yearning upon America her son

Returned to love and bless her ; thanking Heaven,
Whose overruling wisdom ordereth all things,
Making man's wrath work the good will of God,
That these twin giant peoples linked together
Shall hold both hemispheres in fee between them,
Making the world their one imperial realm !

ACT II.

SCENE 1. — *A Street in Philadelphia.*

[*Enter* TIMOTHY, *meeting* ELDAD *and* NATHAN.]

TIMOTHY.

What of the war up North, good Deacon Eldad.

ELDAD.

It's well begun, friend; and —

TIMOTHY.

Good, — well begun, —
So says poor Richard, well begun, half done.

ELDAD.

Don't you believe it: never a proverb yet
But it's as easily twisted on itself
As any Jonah's gourd, — lo — hearken now,
Rise with the lark and lie down with the lamb, —
Lambs are asleep at noon when the lark rockets;
Do everything to-day and not to-morrow, —
As if you wouldn't be wiser by to-morrow
For knowing surely what to-day brings forth;
The early bird gathers the worm, — but then
That earlier worm were better far abed, —

TIMOTHY.

Well, Deacon, don't be tedious, — how's the war?

ELDAD.

Friend, I must end my homily on beginnings:
It is a simple business to begin;
But to go on, and on, and persevere
Wrestling down Amaleks, and fording Jordans,
And wandering wearily the sandy flats
Of some hot wilderness, not half way yet,
Oh, not half midway yet, — here is the toil,
I tell you —

TIMOTHY.

Well but, Deacon, how's the war?

ELDAD.

It's well begun, I grant it, well begun;
Something is done, though much remains to do,
And thus —

[*Enter* JOHN ADAMS.]

TIMOTHY TO JOHN ADAMS.

From Boston, sir? how goes the war?

JOHN ADAMS.

Bravely : at Lexington first blood was drawn;
Pitcairn attacked us; but we answered him
So stoutly, that we drove him for six miles
(He thrice our force and we undisciplined)
Hunting him to his ships at Charlestown Neck,
Where he took shelter with his grenadiers,
Leaving the victory ours.   Massachusetts
Flung out the watchword ' Death or Liberty '
And everywhere the beacons blazed defiance

From State to State through thirteen colonies:
Then the great giant woke, and stood up strong:
A mighty people flaming red with rage.
Gathered by drum and trumpet everywhere:
The steeples clashed to arms, — even pious preachers
Stood on their pulpit stairs, calling to arms;
The teamster left his ploughshare in the furrow
And galloped with his horses to the war, —
The yeoman tore his rifle from its case,
The draper leapt across his counter straight
Eager to fight for freedom; even women
Swarmed in as volunteers, and very children
Shouldered the muskets they could scarcely lift.
We soon had thirty thousand men in arms,
Selected from three hundred thousand more,
And at their head our noble Washington,
Chosen Commander-in-Chief.

TIMOTHY.

Good news; what more?

JOHN ADAMS.

On Lake Champlain, Arnold and Ethan Allen,
From Vermont, with their brave Green Mountain Boys,
Surprised Ticonderoga and Crownpoint,
Seizing their stores of cannon, and supplies —

TIMOTHY.

Good, good, ey Deacon, — well begun half done?

JOHN ADAMS.

And though at Bunker's Hill we failed at first,
Through lack of powder for our empty guns,

Yet those few cartridges had burnt so well
The enemy fell before us in such heaps
They conquered but a fatal victory.
Then Washington rushed fiercely to the front
And shelled them from the heights of Dorchester,
And stormed them out of Boston in hot haste,
Howe and his veteran army in a mass
Driven to his ships by Putnam's bayonets.
Enough — the right is conquering — fare you well.

Exit John Adams.

TIMOTHY.

Well, Deacon Eldad, what say you to this —
Is well begun, half done? —

ELDAD.

Nay, Timothy,
You count the profits only; take your ledger
And post me up the loss; I wot the loss,
Could we but count it, balances the gain,
Ay, much outweighs it, — look you firstly, now —

TIMOTHY.

Deacon, I cannot stop; for firstly means
Secondly, thirdly, and fifteenthly too, —

ELDAD.

But, Haerlem Heights? Kip's Bay? call you these
       gains,
Where Washington gave orders to shoot down
Our many runaways? Then Hackensack —

TIMOTHY.

Croaker! be dumb: or shout at Trenton Falls
With conquering Washington, Their flags are struck!
No more.   Good den, good Deacon.

Exit.

ELDAD.

Well, methinks
Folks are gone mad, they will not listen to reason;
The love of liberty hath driven them mad;
There is some fighting fever in the air
Tainting us all with a contagious courage :
I should not wonder now, if Nathan and I
Were some day found shouldering a firelock too,
And shouting after General Washington.

SCENE 2.

A Chamber.   Patrick Henry and Washington.

PATRICK HENRY.

We can rejoice together, General,
That our own dear Virginia joined the league,
Albeit at bloody cost already; — Norfolk,
That loyal town of peaceful homes, burnt down
By the cold cowardly despot Lord Dunmore,
Who hiding on a man-of-war in the roads
Dared thus to cannonade us! — O King George,
If Cæsar had his Brutus, Charles his Cromwell,
'Twere well you — profited — I say no more —
By such examples.

WASHINGTON.

　　　　　　This is saddening news; —
Friend, I have more to make me sorrowful.
New York is falling away; Connecticut
Is wearying as half-hearted in the cause,
Her levies at our need deserting us
Even by battalions, — they had served their year
And must get home they say, — let others fight!
O Sir, my soul has groaned, where are the men
With whom I must defend America? —
The weight of care lies heavy on my heart
Shamed by desertions, vexed with meannesses,
The jealousy of Congress and the taunts
"Even of brother soldiers slandering me.

PATRICK HENRY.

I hear that General Lee has brought a charge
Of sloth, incompetence, I know not what —

WASHINGTON.

O Sir, the worst afflictions of a man
Come from false friends, envious competitors
Whispering detraction in a private sense,
More than from public foes: I can endure
Defeat, but not defection; all the toils,
Perils and open accidents of war,
But not the secret jealousies of peace.
They thwart me, doubt me, misinterpret me,
Maligning all that's done, and left undone.
I may stand up serene, but feel it still.

PATRICK HENRY.

For climax, Colonel Reed, your secretary,
Stings you, 'tis said, with slander.

WASHINGTON.

        Yes, — I know it;
Pass him; forget it all, I can forgive,
I will not even let him know I know it:
Trust me, — and let me drop it lightly thus,
As not to be down-tilted by a reed.

PATRICK HENRY.

Cheerfully taken: the well balanced mind
However hemmed by adverse circumstance
As in a labyrinth of cactus hedges
Is always happy in itself, at peace
And ready thus to beat down to its will
The thorns of still opposing circumstance.
We count and call you, George, our Fabius,
Winning by patience what with all your skill,
With all your courage, hangs still in the balance
Unwon, and not to be won, save by waiting:
In war, in peace, the name of Washington
Lives in all hearts and dwells upon all tongues,
At once our Fabius and our Hannibal.

WASHINGTON.

Peace, friend, no praising; any speech but that:
The man who knows himself can bear reproach
Better than flattery: do I call you flatterer?
Forgive me this sharp word, dear Patrick Henry, —

I know your soul sincere: yet, while my thanks
Are yours for so much love, suffer my foes
To speak their thoughts of me for good or evil:
Cæsar and Curtius are my teachers here;
A man is nothing if he has no foes,
Nothing, if slander, ridicule, contempt
Are not the frequent scorpions in his path;
Can he have lived a life of faithfulness
Of earnest work for good, and have escaped
Hatred from wickedness, or scorn from folly?
No, — there are serpents still hissing before him:
Let him march on, as duty bids, unfearing,
And trample out their poison as he goes;
Let him march on, heedless of praise and censure,
Living alone for conscience and for God,
And he shall make his veriest foes his friends.
I have stood up well nigh alone thou knowest,
Daring impossibles to save the state,
That scarce will let me save it; thus I reap
The tares of slander sown by factious tongues.
But — I must leave you: I have much to do
And little time for speech.

Exit.

PATRICK HENRY.

Farewell, great heart:
The Saul and the Musæus of our millions.
A nobler spirit never breathed in man;
Thoughtful for others, and forgetting self,
Dauntless in danger, yet so meek withal;
Calm amid calumnies, and flatteries;
Strengthened through failure, humbled by success,

And full of love for man and trust in God,
Chivalric wise and pious and serene,
The pinnacle of human excellence.
Yes, — I have noted him from earliest youth
And marvelled to what great and lofty ends
The hand of Providence was training him.
He was our Moses in the wilderness
Inured to savage warfare, and prepared
Through perils multitudinous to lead
This people to their Canaan of the West:
And when Monongahela's bloody swamp
Proved gallant Braddock's grave, young Washington
Screened by the Manitou himself, they said,
Alone stood victor on that fatal field;
And ever since the same impetuous soul,
Calm, truthful, bold, upright, and self-reliant,
That dwells within his tall athletic frame
Has marked him out to all a chief of men
Fitted and trained to his high destiny,
The first in peace and war, first everywhere,
First in the hearts of all his countrymen.

Exit.

SCENE 3. — *A Street in Baltimore.*

Enter TIMOTHY, RACHEL, *and* NATHAN; *then* FRANK-
LIN.

TIMOTHY.

It was a day of days, I promise you,
A sight of sights, our Yankee flag's new birth,
At Boston, Dorchester heights, on New Year's Day.

RACHEL.

Yankee — why Yankee?

TIMOTHY.
Yenghees, Redman English.

RACHEL.

But we're not English now.

TIMOTHY.
Who told you that?
We're Greater Britain, England magnified,
In origin and laws and soul the same.
What language do you speak?   Who were your
    fathers?
What's your religion, if not Protestant?
Your books, your liberties, your stalwart force
Of independent character, all English;
They fill an island, we a continent;
We are republicans, they monarchists;
But our Head Man looks very like a King,
And their great Ruler is the sovereign people!
The name seems well enough, our Yankee flag.

RACHEL.

You saw it, Timothy?

TIMOTHY.
Yes, girl, at Boston;
There first was shown that glorious flag unfurled.

NATHAN.

Yea, friend, I too stood by when they tore down
The Union Jack of England and flung out
Those stars and stripes: tell me why stars and stripes.

TIMOTHY.

It's fair enough; they make a pretty show
Shining and wriggling in the sun like snakes.

NATHAN.

That's a poor answer: why choose stripes and stars?

Enter FRANKLIN.

O here comes one can tell us everything.
Goodmorrow, brother Franklin: dost thou know,
And wilt thou say, why they chose stars and stripes?

FRANKLIN.

Yes, Nathan, I proposed it to the Congress.
It was their leader's old crusading blazon,
Washington's coat, his own heraldic shield.

NATHAN.

Can this be known? and was it not ambition?
A Cromwell come again?

FRANKLIN.

        Listen, good friends:
It is not known, and it was not ambition.
He never heard of it till fixed and done.
For on the spur, when we must choose a flag,
Symbolling independent unity,

We, and not he — all was unknown to him —
Took up his coat of arms, and multiplied
And magnified it every way to this
Our glorious national banner.

        RACHEL.

           Coat of arms?
What was this coat of arms?

        FRANKLIN.

           I'll tell you, friends.
I've searched it out and known it for myself,
When late in England there, at Herald's College,
And found the Washingtons of Wessyngton
In County Durham and of Sulgrave Manor
County Northampton, bore upon their shield
Three stars atop, two stripes across the field,
Gules — that is red — on white, and for the crest
An eagle's head upspringing to the light,
Its motto, Latin, "Issue proveth acts."
The architraves at Sulgrave testify,
As sundry painted windows in the hall
At Wessyngton, this was their family coat.
They took it to their new Virginian home:
And at Mount Vernon I myself have noted
An old cast iron scutcheoned chimney-back
Charged with that heraldry.

        TIMOTHY.

           Well, this is strange,
And no one knows it; surely such a relic
Must soon be cared for, if not worshipped —

FRANKLIN.

Sir,

Causes are soon forgotten; consequents
Quickly close-shadow them as plants their seeds.
I wot I am the first to tell you all
This root and reason for our stars and stripes,
Washington's heraldry.   Farewell.   *Exit.*

NATHAN.

Farewell, we thank thee.

TIMOTHY.

Well, Nathan, this is grand about those stars;
The stars are now thirteen, each star a state
And may soon be thrice that, say thirty-nine,
With "forty stripes, save one," to whip the world !
How say you, Quaker friend?

NATHAN.

Well, I opined
Friend Franklin must have known; and I perceive
That eagle's head hath pulled a body out
Fullfledged as mounting to the higher heaven
Trailing a mantlet cloud of stars and stripes.
I am a man of peace, I love not wars;
Yet were it well that none should strive with me,
Or touch, unless in love, those stars and stripes.

TIMOTHY.

Well said, old Nathan! but we stay too long ;
Come to head quarters, — there are all the news.

ACT III.

SCENE 1. — *A Room in* GOVERNOR ARNOLD'S *House,*
at Westpoint.

ARNOLD, *alone.*

They have disgraced me, publicly, condemned me,
Abused me for the bondage of my debts,
Charged me with fraud, tried me, and punished *me*
The Commandant of Philadelphia
Who kept such generous state, and at such cost,
By open shame and formal reprimand
From Washington's own mouth before the Congress!
I will not bear it,— I will be revenged.
What, — had they all so speedily forgotten
How often I their hero, Benedict Arnold,
Led them to Victory ? — witness my great deeds,
Ticonderoga, Champlain, and Lake George,
Crownpoint, Quebec, St. John's and Montreal!
Testify, Saratoga and my wounds,
Testify, graceless Philadelphia!
What? only shame, ruin, ingratitude
For such exploits — and *me ?* I'll have revenge.
No longer shall this calm cold Washington,
This cruel mouthpiece of America,
Reap what I sow of great and glorious deeds.
Benedict Arnold shall be bought for gold,
Seeing they charge him fraudulent for gold;

Benedict Arnold shall be found a traitor,
Seeing they dare despise him as a patriot.
It shall be done, — revenge.   Ho, sister, sister!

She enters.

ARNOLD.

How? still in tears, as ever, — since the day
I bade you think no more of Major André:
Come, cheerily; I have good news for you,
I bid you seek him out, and bring him hither.

MARY.

O joy, O wonder! — but the peril, brother, —
And why?   O for what cause? he is thy foe,
Thou wilt not do him harm?

ARNOLD.

Tut, silly girl,
I beckon him to me to do us good.

MARY.

But wherefore? how? — and still the peril, brother.

ARNOLD.

There is no peril: I will tell thee how;
The why is mine own secret: bring him hither,
Disguised as I shall counsel, at the time,
And to the place, and in the way I bid you.

MARY.

Thy will, my too stern brother, as of old,
Is for my woman's weakness overstrong;
I must obey; yet give one scruple hearing, —

Is the Why good or evil when replied?
I seem to feel I dare not yet obey
If what thou willest is — I cannot speak
What yet is readable from those fierce eyes —
Is — shall I say? — of ill intent, — my brother.

ARNOLD.

That is my business, child: obey at once:
Bring André here: henceforth he is my friend;
Fear nothing from my sometime enmity,
He shall be now my brother as before ＼
And I will give thee to him as his wife.

MARY.

O joy, O wonder — yet —

ARNOLD.

       Not one word more :
I now command : here take him this sealed letter
       (*he has been writing and now seals it*)
Of full particulars for his private eye;
Mark: not one word to any living soul :
Silence, and secrecy; bring André here,
As I have bade him.

MARY.

       One word, Benedict:
Rachel, my maid, goes with me: not alone,
For this would ill become me, — and thy sister;
I cannot visit at the camp alone, —
It were not seemly so, for honour's sake

ARNOLD.

Honour! both men and women mouth that name
And mean but seeming by it; seemly, true,
Honour is nought but seeming; in the dark
White is as black, and honour just like shame.
However, be it so: going to the camp
Seeming must carry it; take your maid with you;
But, not one word that I have sent you both
Thus to the British quarters; let her think
You meet your ancient lover there, and she
May like to find a new one; not one word
Of me, or of the letter, or disguise.

MARY.

Brother, I go — in fear, and yet — O hope,
O wonder!   *Exit.*

ARNOLD, *alone.*

      So, I'll take the enemy's bribe, — .
This welcome thirty thousand offered me
For yielding up the stronghold in my trust.
O needful gold, O gladly welcome gold
More welcome than to pay those shabby debts
Because it buys me to revenge myself.
Look out, forsworn America! look out
Calmvisaged gentlemanly Washington!
Benedict Arnold shall be master yet
And none shall steal his honour but himself:
Benedict Arnold shall achieve the fame
What though it be — of Judas? — for Revenge!
                                  Exit.

SCENE 2. — WASHINGTON *and his wife: letters are brought in by* BISHOP, *who gives him some, and one to* MARTHA WASHINGTON.

MARTHA WASHINGTON.

Another of those wicked letters George,
From some anonymous slanderer; it says —

WASHINGTON.

Nay, — good wife, wise wife — heed not what it says;
Tear it up; if I neither see it nor hear it,
Calumny, like the scorpion when self-stung,
Perishes harmlessly: I will not read it.

MARTHA WASHINGTON.

But our dear Patrick Henry sends it here
That you with him may guess or know the writer;
He fancies him a certain famous Doctor.

WASHINGTON.

Nonsense; I'll have no fancies.

MARTHA WASHINGTON.

But he adds,
It is important, for a duplicate
Was laid before the Congress, and it said —

WASHINGTON.

I care not, Martha, what it said; if Congress
Is capable of listening secretly
To taunts against me, I will answer it
On charges openly brought.

MARTHA WASHINGTON.

    Yet, Patrick Henry,
That friend and brother who is half thy soul,
Asks me to read you this: " The nation needs
" A Joshua, not our loitering Fabius,
" A Conway, Mifflin, Gates, a North, a Lee,
" And not this vacillating Washington:
" Under so weak a leader we must perish,
" Having no chance for victory but in change."
Dear Patrick haply lets you know of this,
Suggesting stronger efforts; for he adds, —
Our friend knows well how wise it is to learn
Even from foes: I spoke up stoutly for him,
Urging, and truly, that if he was weak,
It was in men, in stores, in sinews of war,
Not in the muscle of his own strong soul;
If he was lingering to assure great ends
It was for Congress to ensure full means, —

WASHINGTON.

He spoke but truth; there seldom is a slander
But in some particle was justified.
Factions and parsimony tie me down,
Forcing me to delays against my will.
Enough: let history, and my country's love,
In spite of whisperers and conspirators,
Vindicate Washington to after ages.
Let me hear nothing more of this, dear love.
        (*Enter* BISHOP.)

BISHOP.

Please you, my master, there's a young man here,
Timothy Brown, of Boston, asks to see you.

WASHINGTON.

He may come in.

Enter TIMOTHY.

Your errand: to the point.

TIMOTHY.

General, I want a little word in private.

WASHINGTON.

Speak it; we are alone: only my wife.

TIMOTHY.

I ran down straight from Westpoint over there
To tell your honour what a friend of mine,
Miss Arnold's waiting-maid, has overheard
Her master saying —

WASHINGTON.

And you dared to come
With eavesdroppings to me from a false servant?

MARTHA WASHINGTON.

Yet, hear him, George: speak out, young man, what
is it?

TIMOTHY.

She said, she thought her master was unsafe, —

WASHINGTON.

You say, she thought; you said, she overheard.

TIMOTHY.

She well might think of what she overheard.

WASHINGTON.

I cannot listen to a treacherous tale:
Go: and be silent.

MARTHA WASHINGTON.

Tell me what it was.

TIMOTHY.

She heard him talking of some money-bribe,
And swearing at his wrongs, and threatening ven-
        geance
Against America and Washington.

WASHINGTON.

I'll not believe it! Arnold? General Arnold?
Our staunchest patriot since the war began,
The hero of a hundred well-fought fields, —
Incredible — impossible. Young man,
You hope to be rewarded for this tale:
Leave me; without one word: and take with you
My stern rebuke for having dared to breathe
Slander against a noble name.   (*Exit* TIMOTHY.)
                    Dear wife,
To prove full confidence, I call with you
On Governor Arnold at Westpoint to-pay.
Bishop, — the saddlehorses in an hour.   (*Exeunt.*)

SCENE 3.—*A narrow slip of road or lane.   Enter at opposite points, dressed for travel, meeting and passing each other,* TIMOTHY *and* RACHEL.   *They turn back.*

TIMOTHY.

A pretty mess you've got me into, girl,
By tittletattling.

RACHEL.

I? who tittletattled?

TIMOTHY.

Why, what you told me I have told the General,
And —

RACHEL.

So 'twas you that tittletattled, then?

TIMOTHY.

Ay, but I only said what I'd been told.

RACHEL.

And that's the way all gossip gets abroad:
O Master Timothy, I'm ashamed of you
To charge poor innocent me with tittletattle,
When you were tittletattling all the while.

TIMOTHY.

Well, Rachel, say no more; let us part friends;
I got enough, I tell you, from the General,
So, make it up; I'm going; just one kiss.

RACHEL.

One kiss indeed!

TIMOTHY.

Then, Rachel, I'll take two!

RACHEL.

Adone: — Now, Timothy I must be gone,
My mistress waits; there, — well then I'll forgive you,

(They kiss again)

Now don't go tittletattling about me.

Exeunt opposite.

SCENE 4. — *Major André's Tent, open in front: he has an order book in his hand.*

CORPORAL THOMPSON *comes in and says*

Major, a pair of as pretty country girls
As ever one set eyes on, are along,
And want to see your honour: shall I say
Your honour is engaged?

ANDRÉ, *aside.*

Engaged? ay, once
I might have said so; but that day's gone by. —
By all means, Corporal, bring them: double luck!
A pretty couple truly; well, my girls, —

Enter MARY ARNOLD *and her maid: he starts to see her.*

ANDRÉ.

My beauty! what? it seems a thousand years
Since I set eyes on thee: come in, my beauty!
By what glad chance is it we meet again?

MARY.

My brother Benedict has sent me, John, —

ANDRÉ.

How? Benedict, — he hates us, hang the rebel!

MARY.

Pity him, John; in truth he hates us not,
He bade me tell you that he loves you well,
And all is changed with him, and we may meet
As freely and as gladly as of yore;
Here is his letter.

ANDRÉ.

       Stay, — private and secret, —
Then you know nothing of this note, my pet.

MARY.

No, John, — for he looked stern and would not tell
    me, —
But Rachel here coming along with me
Has told me something strange she over-heard, —

(ANDRÉ *meanwhile is reading the letter — and* COR-
    PORAL THOMPSON *speaking with* RACHEL.)

ANDRÉ.

So; — he is changed indeed; more luck for us:
He bids me call and meet him in two hours

With you, and in civilian dress; — as it were
Your cousin, or your lover, if you will,
An any dare to ask you.

MARY.

But, dear John,
So loved, so long betrothed, tell me the truth;
On what strange errand are we bound, and why
This secrecy, this silence, this disguise.

ANDRÉ.

Would it be like a soldier's honour, Mary,
To tell another man's confided secret?

MARY.

Nay, then, I cannot ask it; yet I fear, —
My heart misgave me at his strange wild eyes,
He will not, cannot, dare not harm thee, dearest?

ANDRÉ.

Fear nothing, darling: we will go together, —
You are my guardian angel, and my strength
Let it suffice for both —
But wait awhile,
It is so long since you and I looked love,
I cannot spare those glances yet, my beauty.
So, we shall soon be married?   Blush again, —
You look so pretty: bid yon maid of yours
Go for a walk with Corporal Thompson there,
They seem already to have had much to say, —
And stay with me awhile, my pretty one —

MARY.

O John — I dare not say. — No! Major André, —
It were too sweet and perilous a joy
To stop one moment longer, — fare thee well:
I and my maid must leave at once: that letter
Tells all my brother's mind; I know not aught:
Farewell, — no more — we meet at Benedict's.

(*Exit.*)

ANDRÉ.

Gone! like a flash of joy and love and beauty!
Well, well; fortune of war: look at this life,
What a continual shift of scenes it is,
Sunshine and storm and good and evil mingled:
And here's a sudden change in that strange man
My would-be brother both in law and arms:
What can it mean? — That he has been disgraced,
Is deep in debt, and hates George Washington,
All this he tells me straight; and more, he writes
That for a good round sum, say forty thousand,
He, their last brigadier, and commandant
Of their stronghold on the Hudson at Westpoint,
Will give it up to Clinton with all stores
And guns and arms and garrison complete,
An easy netful, prisoners of war!
This is too good to be true; here, Corporal Thompson,
I'm going on private business to New York
As a civilian, not in uniform:
No one need know it. By the way, Corporal,
Did those red lips you seemed so taken with
Tell you upon what possible errand came
Her mistress to my quarters.

CORPORAL.

Never a word:
We did but guess your honour's liking to her.

ANDRÉ.

Not a bad guess. — I'm gone for half an hour:
Bring me those clothes for change outside the lines.

(*Exit.*)

CORPORAL.

As if I couldn't guess more truths than one;
As if that little vixen didn't guess,
As if she didn't whisper all she guessed:
Well, — since the Major is no friend of mine
(I had been sergeant but he keeps me servant)
Let him look out: if money's to be got
I'll try to touch some too; master and man
Poor Richard calls them kin! — ay and he says
Forewarned, forearmed: Should General Washington
Hear from me of my Major and his friend,
I'd get a bag o' guineas for my news.

(*Exit.*)

SCENE 5. — *Washington's Quarters. Aides-de-Camp and
Orderlies go in and out: he at a desk with papers.*

WASHINGTON.

Take this despatch with speed to General Greene.
Send General Prescott here.

Your horse can gallop,
Bid General Sullivan bring his forces up
With his best speed.
                    This goes to General Morgan,
I want his rifles quickly to the front.
This to Westpoint.   Less hurry, but due care.
    The Aide, young Custiss, to whom he gives it, says
My General, was that true?

WASHINGTON.

                    Wretchedly true:
I went myself to the fortress; they had fled,
That traitor and that spy; the first escaped
On board a British gunboat in the Hudson,
The other, caught with maps and plans upon him,
Has been condemned to death: a drum-courtmartial
Sentence him to be hanged, — hanged as a spy.

BISHOP.

Can Master speak with a petitioner?

WASHINGTON.

I am engaged: upon what matter? urgent?

BISHOP.

She says, on life or death.

WASHINGTON.

                    A woman then?

ORDERLY.

Yes, General, she would not be denied,
Assured that you would speak with Mary Arnold.

WASHINGTON.

The traitor's sister!   O the bitter pang
That I have lived to call my lifelong friend,
Brother of my first love, as boy and girl,
My lowland beauty of those halcyon days,
A Traitor blackest dyed.

(*To* BISHOP.)
Let her come in.

Aside.   She cannot yet have heard of his escape,
And comes to plead for him: it will be pleasure
However mixed with pain, to let her know
He got off in the Vulture.   Franklin says
There is a spot of calm centering the midst
Of the most furious hurricane ; these toils
And cares of war still find a heart of peace
Serene and quiet in their whirl; —

To his Orderlies, &c.

One moment,
Give space, and leave me : in the corridor
Be ready to my call.   Speed these despatches :

he gives a second batch.

I will give audience to this lady alone.

Enter MARY ARNOLD.

WASHINGTON.

Well, Mary Arnold ; only two short minutes
Can these my thousand cares afford : be quick.

MARY.

O, Sir, there yet is time, — is there yet time?
General, by all the love you bore me once

Spare him, — he must not die, so brave, so young,
So loved, so noble, — say he shall not die!

WASHINGTON.

Mary, it is a melancholy pleasure
To tell thee that he lives, and shall not die, —
The traitor will not meet his doom, — take comfort,
Thy brother has escaped.

MARY.

        O, not my brother !
I do not plead for him : he is our shame, —
Myself I could have stabb'd him for his treason ;
I pray for one less guilty — and more dear —
Betrayed as you were by that villain Benedict,
My own betrothed, my all but husband, André !

WASHINGTON.

How? That mean spy thy husband? I had hoped,
Poor Mary Arnold, to have gladdened thee,
My unknown passionflower of hot sixteen,
For sake of all the past, by the true news
That thy bad brother saves his shameful life :
But this unworthy plea for Major André
Cannot be heard one moment : — he must die.

MARY.

Not yet, not yet ! O spare that precious life !

WASHINGTON.

The spy by all our laws of war must die,
And fourteen officers, the court of trial,

Have given unanimous vote that he be hanged.
I cannot help the matter if I would :
Justice commands and policy commends
No death less utterly shameful for a spy.

MARY.

Yet spare, if not his life, at least his honour.

WASHINGTON.

Honour ? what honour is there in a spy?

MARY.

In some sort it was duty, — he was betrayed, —
He looked for better ends to those worse means ;
The way seemed crooked, but the goal was straight, —

WASHINGTON.

Those who do ill that good may come, poor pleader,
Are caught in their own toils, and swiftly earn
Fit payment for such tortuous policy.
Enough.   I cannot hear one word.   Farewell.
However I may pity him, or thee,
And with whatever sorrow for his doom,
He dies ! a terrible warning, gibbeted
On Westpoint battlements.

*She swoons away, he summons the attendants, and the Act
ends.*

ACT IV.

SCENE 1. — WASHINGTON'S *Camp at Valley Forge:*
he lies on a couch sick of a fever, tended by his wife,
and by BISHOP, *his bodyservant.*

WASHINGTON.

How my poor soldiers must be suffering, wife,
In this hard winter, — shame upon the Congress
That their conflicting factious jealousies
Leave these true patriots perishing of cold
And hunger and disease, unshod, ill clad,
Watching on cold bleak ice-fringed river banks,
Sleeping in snow-wreaths, naked and half starved,
Destitute in this agueish fever swamp !
Yet is their spirit unbroken, — gallant hearts, —
And still they stand with me for liberty.
O wife, it is not on the battle-field
With all its thrilling energetic joys
Where the hotblooded wound is never felt
Nor known until it stiffens and is sore,
But in the weary noisome hospital
The soldier is most tried ; there is his patience,
There is his grandest calmest courage seen, —
More truly even than at Trenton Falls
Where we joined battle with those furious Hessians.

Good wife, you have been the rounds : how fare they
   all,
My noble poor sick fellows ?

MARTHA WASHINGTON.
                          The reports
Are better, dearest George, — and I myself
Have tended many of them, as they lay there
Fevered with wounds, or fainting from disease:
And how they blessed me, ev'n unworthy me,
While I pass'd on between those squalid litters
Dropping the smile of hope, the look of love,
The word of faith in prayer! Husband, we know
There is a force more potent than all drugs
In faithful, earnest, and affectionate prayer.

WASHINGTON.

The best of remedies, in all men's reach:
How often has its potency sufficed
To cure my sharpest pains, most aching cares.
Well may we praise for having leave to pray.

MARTHA WASHINGTON.

Now; — now I am come back to be your nurse,
I cannot let you talk, — it is high time
To take this sleeping draught; and I must urge
The doctor's orders, — quiet.

BISHOP *comes in and says,*
Please you, my Master, there's a woman here,
I'd said a madwoman, would speak with you,
She says her name is Arnold, and her errand
One word alone, — only one word, she says.

WASHINGTON.

Arnold ? — his sister again ? can it then be
That double traitor thinks to serve himself
By some new treachery ? — I abhor ill means;
Hands foul as his shall never help my country;
Yet, hapless Mary Arnold, I will see her,
If only to show kindness and forgive,
As sick men should; she too may well forgive
What duty, painful duty, forced me to,
Hanging her paramour, that wretched spy.

To BISHOP.

Let her come in.

MARTHA WASHINGTON.

Now husband, be advised,
You can see no one yet; the ague fit
Will soon be on you, dearest, — say not yet.

WASHINGTON.

I feel your faithful love, and love you for it;
But let it be:

To BISHOP.

She may come in.

Enter MARY ARNOLD, *in deep mourning, cloaked.*

MARY.

Alone, —
I said — alone, only one word, alone.
General, I have a message to deliver,
But we must be alone.

WASHINGTON.

       None but my wife,
My angel always watching over me,
The more that I am sick and weak.

MARY.

       His wife!
Alone, I prayed only one word alone!

aside. And yet, O chance! O joy! that she shall see
    it!

MARTHA WASHINGTON.

I will not leave my husband, — George, be still, —
No, stay here with his Excellency, Bishop; —
Lady, I speak for him, and I will hear you.
What is your errand? you look wildly on him:
Stand further; — not so near: — can she be mad?

MARY ARNOLD.

I have a message to him from the dead
[Fail not, my hand! be swift and sure my purpose!]
And if not quite alone — it is enough —
This message to his heart!

      (*She rushes to stab him.*)

(MARTHA WASHINGTON *and* BISHOP *struggle with her
    and disarm her.*)

MARTHA WASHINGTON.

Hold her back, Bishop! cruel, murderous wretch, —
Why strike so fiercely at this most precious life?

MARY ARNOLD.

In fierce revenge for a most precious life!
O that I had another dagger here!
Unhand me! let me go! I must away!

WASHINGTON, *rising*.

Let her escape, poor soul! she cannot harm me:
I will be still, dear wife. Take her away (*to Bishop*),
See to her safety well beyond the lines.
Let no one know of this, I charge you both;
Be silent and be faithful: if the camp
Heard of her coming, 'twas some madwoman:
Let no one guess her name, or her intent.

(*They go out.*)

Dear wife, I praise the Overruling Power
That every inch and instant guideth us:
The merest seeming accident is of Him, —
Even the fiercest storms are in His hand;
Let us walk straightway on the path of duty
Trusting in God, no shot or shell can strike us,
No poison sap our life, no murderous steel
Summon us to His throne before our time, —
Quiet? — I will be quiet, dear, dear wife.

(*Sits down*)

MARTHA WASHINGTON.

Here, slumber awhile, — thy head upon my breast;
I trust this fright has scattered away the fit.
Rest thee: no sleeping draught? well —

WASHINGTON.

Precious wife,
I will be quiet; yet it calms me more

To speak than to be silent: that poor woman
[God show more mercy to her than man has shown !]
Let none attempt to seize or punish her.
If you forgive her, it will cheer my sadness.

MARTHA WASHINGTON.

For thy sake, at thy word, but only so, —
Be it, — that I forgive her; yet my husband,
Think what America had lost in thee
If that mad wretch had murdered Washington!

WASHINGTON.

Heaven ordered otherwise: all is guided well:
Still are my fortunes and America's
Now at their lowest: I am sad, dear wife;
It is a bitter season now for me;
Both foes and friends malign me ; General Gates
Whose triumph northward I have helped so well,
Has turned to be my rival, not my colleague:
I battle on, but under cloudy skies;
And in these dreary swamps of Delaware
Hope grows heartsick: well, even at the worst
With all else failure, at our bitterest need,
May Heaven's High Providence yet grant Success!
                        (*An Orderly comes in.*)

ORDERLY.

General, a well attended gentleman
Lately from France, the Marquis of La Fayette,
Craves audience.

WASHINGTON.

Let him come in.

(he rises.

I thank my God!
Scarce can we breathe a prayer, He answereth us:
Herein I hail the dawn of brighter things,
France and America in glad alliance!

(They come in.)

I bid you welcome, Sirs; yet you may see
How woefully we speed here in these marshes.
Not but that hope is ours, hope, no despair,
But stout determined courage and endurance
Yea to the end, Triumph and good success!

LA FAYETTE.

Your Excellency, let a fervent heart
Bring sunshine to your quarters with good news,
France sends a fleet and army on your side
Standing for you and liberty : these friends,
Admiral De Grasse, St. Simon, Rochambeau,
Haste here to cheer you.

WASHINGTON.

Thanks, good gentlemen ;
From my poor country, thanks ; from this dear wife
[My brave companion greets you courteously]
And from my humbler self, thanks, gentlemen.
Indeed the dawn is breaking while we speak,
The darkness vanishes, mists melt away ;
I see new hopes, like distant hilltops bright
As with the morning sun, — America

Yet, yet, thou shalt be Free ; that happy thought
Glows at my heart, and fills it with new power,
Liberty smiling on this golden hour!

> *They go out together.*

SCENE 2. —*Changes to a Street in Baltimore.*

*A crowd of recruits come in, armed variously and with
the national flag; among them Eldad and Nathan, with
muskets and ridiculous attempts at uniform, spectacled,
&c.*

> *Opposite, enter* TIMOTHY.

TIMOTHY.

Can I believe my eyes ?   Why, Deacon, Deacon,
Do I see straight that this is you, — and Nathan ?
Dear simple souls, how got you in this guise ?

NATHAN.

I do opine this is myself — and Eldad ;
Touching the firelocks, good Timothy,
I trow we somehow manage shouldering them
But as to loading them, or drawing trigger —

ELDAD.

Verily, neighbour, we were forced to come,
That is, we liked not to be left behind
When everyone was mustering to the war

With guns and swords, and scythes and pitchforks too,
Saying they had caught the British in a trap
Down south at York Town, — much as with Burgoyne
Up north at Saratoga, Gage at Boston,
And divers other pitfalls —

TIMOTHY.

Deacon Eldad, —
Come to the point — *you* are the text, not others.

ELDAD.

As I was just expounding, we were forced,
Nathan and I — not to be left behind.
For all the folk were pressing hitherward,
And the whole country, like a swarm of ants,
Is black and red and blue and white with life,
Horsemen and footmen, cannon, carts, and stores,
All to one point converging in such streams
We couldn't help but come, — ey, brother Nathan ?

NATHAN.

Speak for thyself : I could, but would not, help it, —
What stirred me up in spirit was the shame
That mercenary Hessians should be here
Killing and burning ; so I asked myself,
Nathan, shall such things be, — Nathan said Nay, —
And forthwith did I buy me this good gun ;
If any friend will show me how to load it,
I'll dare to pull that trigger on a Hessian !

TIMOTHY.

Bravo, my gallant Quaker ! here's a change, —
The patriot flame flashes from heart to heart
Till even the coldest feels that glorious heat !
None can escape the wholesome happy fever.

(to the recruits)

What say you, countrymen, — are you prepared
To fight to the last gasp for liberty ?

(they shout)

Ay, ay, All of us, every man of us !

TIMOTHY.

Then come along in line — I'll be your serjeant,
Company ! atten-shun ! — right about face !
Step, left foot forward, maarch !   *(they go out.)*
                    I'll teach you, Nathan,
The drill of that same rifle, come with me;
As for you, Deacon Eldad —

(Nathan and Timothy go out.)

ELDAD, *alone.*

                    As for me,
I daren't be left behind, good Timothy,
I'll make what speed I can, for firstly, I —

*(looking round and finding himself alone, he
limps after them with all speed.)*

I should have told him of my rheumatism ! —

Exit.

ACT V.

The lines near York Town.   Washington and Staff, &c.

JOHN ADAMS.

The lion is in your toils at last then, General.
After his raid upon the Carolines
And through Virginia, Greene has hunted him,
And Morgan driven him hard and hemmed him in
To this peninsula between two rivers,
The York and the James; he has no chance of escape;
For Count De Grasse blockades him from the sea,
And Rochambeau pushes him on the left,
Your veteran levies close upon his right,
The country up in arms is crowded round him,
Our parallels and trenches block him in,
The cannons battering him on every side, —
He must surrender.

WASHINGTON.

                    Yes, comrade and statesman,
My brother in the council and the field,
The Lord Cornwallis with seven thousand men,
Surrounded by our forces and shut up
Helplessly here in York Town, must surrender.
All day, all night, our murderous batteries
Have shattered his defences, and he must
Either be butchered there, or lower his flag.

The God of Christian battles is no Moloch:
The less of carnage in a victory
The more of glory.   Could he but surrender,
He should have honourable terms: his ships
Lie out at sea beyond De Grasse's fleet;
Would he were safe on board them, homeward bound,
Leaving us free and independent! — Schuyler,
Go up to York Town with a flag of truce
And say that in America's great name
And for the cause of just humanity,
Washington offers terms; the Lord Cornwallis
In token of submission yields his sword;
All other officers and men retain
Their arms and colours, — cased and not unfurled —
Save a few standards left for trophy here, —
They leave their guns and stores, but for all else
They may march out paroled, with honours of war.

LA FAYETTE.

Are not these terms, forgive me, General,
Too easy for a foe so crushed and fallen?

WASHINGTON.

Nay, noble friend! because he is so crushed
It well becomes us to deal generously
And gently with him: more than this, dear Marquis,
I cannot wish to trample down in shame
The honour of my whilome country England;
Yea, could I claim disgraceful terms, I know
That not one man of all the thousands there
But would be blown to pieces where he stood

Rather than yield to terms not honourable.
An Englishman will render up his life,
But not his honour.   Therefore General Schuyler,
Go with these terms to York Town.

(he goes.)

Gallant Marquis,
We owe so much to you and to your country
That I shall ask you to receive the sword
Of Lord Cornwallis; haply all the fitter
For that he once scoffed at your beardless youth,
Goliath-like with David.   Take this honour.

La Fayette.

No, General Washington, the right is yours;
On your own soil a conquering patriot
You must be first in peace as first in war:
I pray your Excellency, conclude this triumph.

Washington.

Thou noble nature!—yet, one better thought;
It happened that at Charleston General Lincoln
Lately gave up his sword to Lord Cornwallis;
I trust your courteous heart discerns his right
(Since your own modesty renounces it)
To reap as thus his honourable revenge,
By standing in my stead: when all is done,
Let Lincoln for America take the sword.

Franklin.

Ever unselfish! like George Washington!
Look: General Schuyler, just as he set out,

Has met the enemy's counter flag of truce,
Asking for terms! O happy interchange,
If righteousness and peace can kiss each other,
And England and America be one
Through Washington their bond of unity!

JOHN ADAMS.

Has the Chief heard how dangerously lies sick
His gallent stepson Custiss in the trenches?

WASHINGTON.

I know it, sadly; fever, — nigh unto death;
So closely sorrow cuts the heels of joy.
I came here from him straight, returning straightway;
Meanwhile his mother and our skilful friend
The good physician Craik, watch by the couch.
I trust in heaven to guide us all for the best.
See to these few last orders. Dear La Fayette,
Loved by me as a father loves his son,
When those few trophy standards are brought in
Accept a pair to take with you to France,
America's gift of honour: Rochambeau
And Count La Grasse, and noble Baron Steubel,
Let each of them receive like gifts of honour;
One stack of colours we will keep for home
To decorate our future Capitol:
The rest may England, once our foe, take back.
Bid General Lincoln, having touched the hilt
Of Lord Cornwallis's sword, sealing submission,
Restore it straightway, with due courtesy:
So would we conquer in all kindliness.

And now, friends, give me leave to say farewell:
My work in life is done, my part is played;
At last, at last, in peace I lay me down
Wearied of strife and factions: from henceforth
Like Cincinnatus, at my Sabine farm,
Treading the tranquil path that leads to Heaven,
By the Potomac, like its stream, my life
Shall flow down gently to the sleep of death.

PATRICK HENRY.

No, Sir! your country cannot spare you yet,
Obscurely couched on the soft lap of home;
America has still a thousand needs
You only can supply: and there be some
(As Colonel Nicol and the army in mass)
Already dream to hail you our first King, —
An you be willing.

WASHINGTON.

                    King? — it cannot be, —
It must not, shall not be! I to be King?
The army to be tyrant of this people?
I to be thought so base as to desire
To trample on my countrymen as King?
I hate the very name, the very thought!
Some Kings may have been good; but most were evil;
For rank is as a poison to the man,
Rotting his virtues by presumptuous pride.
No! Patrick Henry, we have fought too well,
Too fiercely for an end so low as this,
The leprous badge of worn-out monarchy,

Blighting our free America with Kings: —
Never will I stand other as your chief,
If chief at all, than plain George Washington,
Happier to farm afield than fight afield.
Tell all those flatterers this: no crown for me,
No puppet pride of rank above my fellows,
All equals and all freemen, even as I:
But, if they will so set me in the front
To stand their servant, ministering the law,
As the Republic's head and president,
Simply their President, if the People please,
But neither Highness, — no, nor Excellency, —
Well, — I postpone my homely hope of quiet,
To be your chief in peace as chief in war.

Yes, and I yet may find another mission,
Haply a higher and a wider one;
Whereby in Heaven's good time, near or far off,
When stablished liberty is strong in us,
By me, or my successors, mother and child
May yet be reconciled, renewing loves.
For dear to us, in spite of all her faults,
Is England; and America may hope
Again to seek and bless her as her child.
So, hand in hand, like sisters in a ring,
Round the whole world shall Britain's colonies,
Each independent, but united all,
Even as our own beloved America,
Gladden with freedom Universal Man.

END.

VALUABLE AND INTERESTING WORKS OF HISTORY, BIOGRAPHY
TRAVELS, FICTION, ETC., ETC.

Zenobia; or, The Fall of Palmyra. In Letters of L. MANLIUS
PISO, from Palmyra, to his Friend MARCUS CURTIUS at Rome. By WILLIAM
WARE. 12mo, cloth. Price... $2 00

Aurelian; or, Rome in the Third Century. In Letters of
LUCIUS M. PISO, from Rome, to FAUSTA. the Daughter of GRACCHUS, at
Palmyra. A sequel to "Zenobia." By WILLIAM WARE. 12mo, cloth.
Price............... .... $2 00

Julian; or, Scenes in Judea. By WILLIAM WARE. 12mo, cloth.
Price... .. .. $2 00

"Ancient Classics from the pen of a modern writer. They are fine specimens of that
form of Moral Romance, of which the samples are few—and are most brilliant additions
to American Literature."—*N. A. Review.*

Friends in Council; A Series of Readings and Discourse
Thereon. By ARTHUR HELPS. Complete in two volumes. 12mo, cloth.
Price............... .... $4 00

"It is good, in *Discourse,* and Speech of Conversation, to vary, and intermingle Speech
of the present Occasion with Arguments; Tales with Reasons, Asking of Questions, with
Telling of Opinions; and Jest with Earnest: For it is a dull Thing to Tire, and as we say
now, to Jade, anything too far."—BACON, *Essay of Discourse.*

Sartor Resartus: The Life and Opinions of HERR TEUFELS-
DROCKH. By THOMAS CARLYLE. 12mo, cloth. Price .... 75 cts.

Our New Home In the West; or, Glimpses of Life Among the
Early Settlers. Illustrated by F. O. C. DARLEY. By MRS. C. M. KIRKLAND.
12mo, cloth. Price... .... $1 50

Holidays Abroad; or, Europe from the West. By MRS. C. M.
KIRKLAND. 12mo, cloth. Price.......... ....~..... $2 00

Lavinia; or, One Year of Wedlock. Translated from the Swed-
ish of EMILIE F. CARLEN. 12mo, cloth. Price.................... $1 25

Undine and Sintram. Translated from the German of BARON
FOUQUÉ. 12mo, cloth. Price............. .,............. .... $1 25

Thiodolph, the Icelander. Translated from the German of
BARON FOUQUÉ. 12mo, cloth. Price......... .... $1 25

Artist's Married Life. Being that of ALBERT DÜRER. Trans
lated from the German of LEOPOLD SCHEFER, by MRS. J. R. STODART. Re
vised edition, with a Memoir. 12mo, cloth. Price... ....:... $1 25

Galaxy of Wit and Wisdom; or, Fun for the Million A Choice
Collection of the Humorous Sayings of Tom Hood, Douglas Jerrold, Sher-
idan, Coleman and others. Illustrated. 16mo, cloth. Price....... $1 25

Vathek. An Arabian Tale. By WILLIAM BECKFORD. With
Notes, Critical and Explanatory. 12mo, cloth. Price.............. $1 25

The Romance of a Poor Young Man. Translated from the
French of Octave Feuillet. 12mo, cloth. Price $1 50

PUBLISHED BY JAMES MILLER, 647 BROADWAY.

BEAUTIFUL RED LINE EDITION
OF THE POETS.

SMALL QUARTO, BEVELLED BOARDS, GILT EDGES.

Elizabeth Barrett Browning's Poems.
Illustrated by SOL. EYTINGE, JR., W. J. HENNESSEY, W. THWAITES, and C. G. BUSH. 1 volume, - - - - - $4.50

Aurora Leigh.
By ELIZABETH BARRETT BROWNING. Illustrated by C. G. BUSH, SOL. EYTINGE, JR., and W. J. HENNESSEY. 1 volume, - - $3.50

Thomas Hood's Poems. Complete.
Illustrated by GUSTAVE DORÉ, SOL. EYTINGE, JR., and others. 1 volume, - - $4.50

John Keats' Poems. Complete.
Illustrated by BIRKET FOSTER, WEHNERT, CHAPMAN, and others. 1 volume, - - $3.50

Robert Burns' Poems. Complete.
Illustrated by Eminent English Artists. 1 volume, - - - - - - $4.50

Thomas Campbell's Poems. Complete.
Illustrated by BIRKET FOSTER, HARRISON WEIR, JOHN GILBERT, and others. 1 volume, - - - - - - $3.50

Thomas Gray's Poems. Complete.
Illustrated by BIRKET FOSTER. 1 volume, $3.50

Thomas Babington Macauley's Lays of Ancient Rome.
Illustrated by C. J. BUSH, and others. 1 volume, - - - - - $3.50

STANDARD AND CLASSIC BOOKS,

PUBLISHED BY JAMES MILLER,

647 Broadway, N. Y.

UNDINE AND SINTRAM. Translated from the German of Baron Fouqué. These two classic stories are complete in one volume.
Cloth, black and gold, - - - - - **$1 25**

THIODOLF THE ICELANDER. Translated from the German of the Baron De La Motte Fouqué.
Cloth, black and gold, - - - - - **1 25**

VATHEK. An Arabian Tale. By W. Beckford. With Notes critical and explanatory.
Cloth, black and gold, - - - - - **1 25**

THE EPICUREAN. A Romance. By Thomas Moore.
Cloth, black and gold, - - - - - **1 25**

THINKS I TO MYSELF. A Serio-Ludicro-Tragico Comedy.
One volume, cloth, - - - - - **1 25**

THE ROMANCE OF A POOR YOUNG MAN. Translated from the French of Octave Feuillet.
One volume, cloth, - - - - - **1 50**

ZENOBIA; OR, THE FALL OF PALMYRA. An Historical Romance. By William Ware. New edition. Complete in one volume. With a portrait of the author.
Cloth, - - - - - - - **2 00**

"An ancient classic from the pen of a modern writer. A fine specimen of that form of moral romance, of which the samples are few."—*S. Patriot.*
"One of the most brilliant additions to American literature."—*N. A Review.*

AURELIAN; OR, ROME IN THE THIRD CENTURY A Sequel to Zenobia. By the same author. New edition, to match Zenobia, - - - - - **2 00**

JULIAN; OR, SCENES IN JUDEA. By the author of Zenobia and Aurelian. New edition, to match, - - **2 00**

SECRET HISTORY OF THE FRENCH COURT UNDER RICHELIEU AND MAZARIN. Translated from the French of Victor Cousin.
One volume, cloth, - - - - - **1 25**

www.ingramcontent.com/pod-product-compliance
Lightning Source LLC
Chambersburg PA
CBHW030025030726
47499CB00008B/3124